# EXILE FROM SPACE

Start Publishing PD LLC
Copyright © 2024 by Start Publishing PD LLC



Start Publishing PD is a registered trademark of Start Publishing PD LLC
Manufactured in the United States of America

Cover art: Shutterstock/Taisiya Kozorez

Cover design: Jennifer Do

10  9  8  7  6  5  4  3  2  1

ISBN 979-8-8809-0440-2

# EXILE FROM SPACE

by Judith Merril

*"They" worried about the impression she'd make. Who could imagine that she'd fall in love, passionately, the way others of her blood must have done? Who was this strange girl who had been born in this place—and still it wasn't her home?...*

I don't know where they got the car. We made three or four stops before the last one, and they must have picked it up one of those times. Anyhow, they got it, but they had to make a license plate, because it had the wrong kind on it.

They made me some clothes, too—a skirt and blouse and shoes that looked just like the ones we saw on television. They couldn't make me a lipstick or any of those things, because there was no way to figure out just what the chemical composition was. And they decided I'd be as well off without any driver's license or automobile registration as I would be with papers that weren't exactly perfect, so they didn't bother about making those either.

They were worried about what to do with my hair, and even thought about cutting it short, so it would look more like the women on television, but that was one time I was way ahead of them. I'd seen more shows than anyone else, of course—I watched them almost every minute, from the time they told me I was going—and there was one where I'd seen a way to make braids and put them around the top of your head. It wasn't very comfortable, but I practiced at it until it looked pretty good.

They made me a purse, too. It didn't have anything in it except the diamonds, but the women we saw always seemed to carry them, and they thought it might be a sort of superstition or ritual necessity, and that we'd better not take a chance on violating anything like that.

They made me spend a lot of time practicing with the car, because without a license, I couldn't take a chance on getting into any trouble. I must have put in the better part of an hour starting and stopping and backing that thing, and turning it around, and weaving through trees and rocks, before they were satisfied.

Then, all of a sudden, there was nothing left to do except go. They made me repeat everything one more time, about selling the diamonds, and how to register at the hotel, and what to do if I got into trouble, and how to get in touch with them when I wanted to come back. Then they said good-bye, and made me promise not to stay *too* long, and said they'd keep in touch the best they could. And then I got in the car, and drove down the hill into town.

I knew they didn't want to let me go. They were worried, maybe even a little afraid I wouldn't want to come back, but mostly worried that I might say something I shouldn't, or run into some difficulties they hadn't anticipated. And outside of that, they knew they were going to miss me. Yet they'd made up their minds to it; they planned it this way, and they felt it was the right thing to do, and certainly they'd put an awful lot of thought and effort and preparation into it.

If it hadn't been for that, I might have turned back at the last minute. Maybe they were worried; but *I* was petrified. Only of course, I wanted to go, really. I couldn't help being curious, and it never occurred to me then that I might miss them. It was the first time I'd ever been out on my own, and they'd promised me, for years and years, as far back as I could remember, that some day I'd go back, like this, by myself. But....

Going back, when you've been away long enough, is not so much a homecoming as a dream *deja vu*. And for me, at least, the dream was not entirely a happy one. Everything I saw or heard or touched had a sense of haunting familiarity, and yet of *wrongness*, too—almost a nightmare feeling of the oppressively inevitable sequence of events, of faces and features and events just not-quite-remembered and not-quite-known.

I was born in this place, but it was not my home. Its people were not mine; its ways were not mine. All I knew of it was what I had been told, and what I had seen for myself these last weeks of preparation, on the television screen. And the dream-feeling was intensified, at first, by the fact that I did not know *why* I was there. I knew it had been planned this way, and I had been told it was necessary to complete my education. Certainly I was aware of the great effort that had been made to make the trip possible. But I did not yet understand just *why*.

Perhaps it was just that I had heard and watched and thought and dreamed too much about this place, and now I was actually there, the reality was—not so much a disappointment as—just sort of *unreal*. Different from what I knew when I *didn't* know.

The road unwound in a spreading spiral down the mountainside. Each time I came round, I could see the city below, closer and larger, and less distinct. From the top, with the sunlight sparkling on it, it had been a clean and gleaming pattern of human civilization. Halfway down, the symmetry was lost, and the smudge and smoke began to show.

Halfway down, too, I began to pass places of business: restaurants and gas stations and handicraft shops. I wanted to stop. For half an hour now I had been out on my own, and I still hadn't seen any of the people, except the three who had passed me behind the wheels of their cars, going up the road. One of the shops had a big sign on it, "COME IN AND LOOK AROUND." But I kept going. One thing I understood was that it was absolutely necessary to have money, and that I must stop nowhere, and attempt nothing, till after I had gotten some.

Farther down, the houses began coming closer together, and then the road stopped winding around, and became almost straight. By that time, I was used to the car, and didn't have to think about it much, and for a little while I really enjoyed myself. I could see into the houses sometimes, through the windows, and at one, a woman was opening the door, coming out with a broom in her hand. There were children playing in the yards. There were cars of all kinds parked around the houses, and I saw dogs and a couple of horses, and once a whole flock of chickens.

But just where it was beginning to get really interesting, when I was coming into the little town before the city, I had to stop watching it all, because there were too many other people driving. That was when I began to understand all the fuss about licenses and tests and traffic regulations. Watching it on television, it wasn't anything like being in the middle of it!

Of course, what I ran into there was really nothing; I found that out when I got into the city itself. But just at first, it seemed pretty bad. And I still don't understand it. These people are pretty bright mechanically. You'd think anybody who could *build* an automobile—let alone an atom bomb—could *drive* one easily enough. Especially with a lifetime to learn in. Maybe they just like to live dangerously....

It was a good thing, though, that I'd already started watching out for what the other drivers were doing when I hit my first red light. That was something I'd overlooked entirely, watching street scenes on the screen, and I guess they'd never noticed either. They must have taken it for granted, the way I did, that people stopped their cars out of courtesy from time to time to let the others go by. As it was, I stopped because the others did, and just happened to notice that they began again when the light changed to green. It's really a very good system; I don't see why they don't have them at all the intersections.

* * * * *

From the first light, it was eight miles into the center of Colorado Springs. A sign on the road said so, and I was irrationally pleased when the speedometer on the car confirmed it. Proud, I suppose, that these natives from my own birth-place were such good gadgeteers. The road was better after that, too, and the cars didn't dart in and out off the sidestreets the way they had before. There was more traffic on the highway, but most of them behaved fairly intelligently. Until we got into town, that is. After that, it was everybody-for-himself, but by then I was prepared for it.

I found a place to park the car near a drugstore. That was the first thing I was supposed to do. Find a drugstore, where there would likely be a telephone directory, and go in and look up the address of a hock shop. I had a little trouble parking the car in the space they had marked off, but I could see from the way the others were stationed that you were supposed to get in between the white lines, with the front of the car next to the post on the sidewalk. I didn't know what the post was for, until I got out and read what it said, and then I didn't know what to do, because I didn't *have* any money. Not yet. And I didn't dare get into any trouble that might end up with a policeman asking to see my license, which always seemed to be the first thing they did on television, when they talked to anybody who was driving a car. I got back in the car and wriggled my way out of the hole between the other cars, and tried to think what to do. Then I remembered seeing a sign that said "Free Parking" somewhere, not too far away, and went back the way I'd come.

There was a sort of park, with a fountain spraying water all over the grass, and a big building opposite, and the white lines here were much more sensible. They were painted in diagonal strips, so you could get in and out quite easily, without all that backing and twisting and turning. I left the car there, and remembered to take the keys with me, and started walking back to the drugstore.

*

That was when it hit me.

Up to then, beginning I guess when I drove that little stretch coming into Manitou, with the houses on the hills, and the children and yards and dogs and chickens, I'd begun to feel almost as if I belonged here. The people seemed so *much* like me—as long as I wasn't right up against them. From a little distance, you'd think there was no difference at all. Then, I guess, when I was close enough to notice, driving through town, I'd been too much preoccupied with the car. It didn't really get to me till I got out and started walking.

They were all so *big*....

They were big, and their faces and noses and even the pores of their skin were too big. And their voices were too loud. And they *smelled*.

I didn't notice that last much till I got into the drugstore. Then I thought I was going to suffocate, and I had a kind of squeezing upside-down feeling in my stomach and diaphragm and throat, which I didn't realize till later was what they meant by "being sick." I stood over the directory rack, pretending to read, but really just struggling with my insides, and a man came along and shouted in my ear something that sounded like, "Vvvm trubbb lll-lll-lll ay-dee?" (I didn't get that sorted out for hours afterwards, but I don't think I'll ever forget just the way it sounded at the time. Of course, he meant, "Having trouble, little lady?") But all I knew at the time was he was too big and smelled of all kinds of things that were unfamiliar and slightly sickening. I couldn't answer him. All I could do was turn away so as not to breathe him, and try to pretend I knew what I was doing with the directory. Then he hissed at me ("Sorry, no offense," I figured out later), and said clearly enough so I could understand even then, "Just trying to help," and walked away.

As soon as he was gone, I walked out myself. Directory or no directory, I had to get out of that store. I went back to where I'd left the car, but instead of getting in it, I sat down on a bench in the park, and waited till the turmoil inside me began to quiet down.

I went back into that drugstore once before I left, purposely, just to see if I could pin down what it was that had bothered me so much, because I never reacted that strongly afterwards, and I wondered if maybe it was just that it was the first time I was inside one of their buildings. But it was more than that; that place was a regular snake-pit of a treatment for a stranger, believe me! They had a tobacco counter, and a lunch counter and a perfume-and-toiletries section, and a nut-roasting machine, and just to top it off, in the back of the store, an open-to-look-at (*and* smell) pharmaceutical center! Everything, all mixed together, and compounded with stale human sweat, which was also new to me at the time. And no air conditioning.

Most of the air conditioning they have is bad enough on its own, with chemical smells, but those are comparatively easy to get used to ... and I'll take them *any* time, over what I got in that first dose of *Odeur d'Earth.*

*

Anyhow, I sat on the park bench about fifteen minutes, I guess, letting the sun and fresh air seep in, and trying to tabulate and memorize as many of the components of that drugstore smell as I could, for future reference. I was simply going to have to adjust to them, and next time I wanted to be prepared.

All the same, I didn't feel prepared to go back into the same place. Maybe another store wouldn't be quite as bad. I started walking in the opposite direction, staying on the wide main street, where all the big stores seemed to be, and two blocks down, I ran into luck, because there was a big bracket sticking out over the sidewalk from the front of a store halfway down a side street, and it had the three gold balls hanging from it that I knew, from television, meant the kind of place I wanted. When I walked down to it, I saw too that they had a sign painted over the window: "We buy old gold and diamonds."

Just *how* lucky that was, I didn't realize till quite some time later. I was going to look in the Classified Directory for "Hock Shops." I didn't know any other name for them then.

Inside, it looked exactly like what I expected, and even the smell was nothing to complain about. Camphor and dust and mustiness were strong enough to cover most of the sweaty smell, and those were smells of a kind I'd experienced before, in other places.

The whole procedure was reassuring, because it all went just the way it was supposed to, and I knew how to behave. I'd seen it in a show, and the man behind the grilled window even *looked* like the man on the screen, and talked the same way.

"What can we do for you, girlie?"

"I'd like to sell a diamond," I told him.

He didn't say anything at first, then he looked impatient. "You got it with you?"

"Oh ... yes!" I opened my purse, and took out one of the little packages, and unwrapped it, and handed it to him. He screwed the lens into his eye, and walked back from the window and put it on a little scale, and turned back and unscrewed the lens and looked at me.

"Where'd you get this, lady?" he asked me.

"It's mine," I said. I knew just how to do it. We'd gone over this half a dozen times before I left, and he was behaving exactly the way we'd expected.

"I don't know," he said. "Can't do much with an unset stone like this...." He pursed his lips, tossed the diamond carelessly in his hand, and then pushed it back at me across the counter. I had to keep myself from smiling. It was just the way they'd said it would be. The people here were still in the Mech Age, of course, and not nearly conscious enough to communicate anything at all complex or abstract any way except verbally. But there is nothing abstract about avarice, and between what I'd been told to expect, and what I could feel pouring out of him, I knew precisely what was going on in his mind.

"You mean you don't *want* it?" I said. "I thought it was worth quite a lot...."

"Might have been once." He shrugged. "You can't do much with a stone like that any more. Where'd you get it, girlie?"

"My mother gave it to me. A long time ago. I wouldn't sell it, except.... Look," I said, and didn't have to work hard to sound desperate, because in a way I was. "Look, it must be worth *something*?"

He picked it up again. "Well ... what do you want for it?"

That went on for quite a while. I knew what it was supposed to be worth, of course, but I didn't hope to get even half of that. He offered seventy dollars, and I asked for five hundred, and after a while he gave me three-fifty, and I felt I'd done pretty well—for a greenhorn. I put the money in my purse, and went back to the car, and on the way I saw a policeman, so I stopped and asked him about a hotel. He looked me up and down, and started asking questions about how old I was, and what was my name and where did I live, and I began to realize that being so much smaller than the other people was going to make life complicated. I told him I'd come to visit my brother in the Academy, and he smiled, and said, "Your *brother*, is it?" Then he told me the name of a place just outside of town, near the Academy. It wasn't a hotel; it was a *motel*, which I didn't know about at that time, but he said I'd be better off there. A lot of what he said went right over my head at the time; later I realized what he meant about "a nice respectable couple" running the place. I found out later on, too, that he called them up to ask them to keep an eye on me; he thought I was a nice girl, but he was worried about my being alone there.

By this time, I was getting hungry, but I thought I'd better go and arrange about a place to stay first. I found the motel without much trouble, and went in and registered; I knew how to do that, at least—I'd seen it plenty of times. They gave me a key, and the man who ran the place asked me did I want any help with my bags.

"Oh, no," I said. "No, thanks. I haven't got much."

I'd forgotten all about that, and they'd never thought about it either! These people always have a lot of different clothes, not just one set, and you're supposed to have a suitcase full of things when you go to stay anyplace. I said I was hungry anyway, and wanted to go get something to eat, and do a couple of other things—I didn't say what—before I got settled. So the woman walked over with me, and showed me which cabin it was, and asked was everything all right?

It looked all right to me. The room had a big bed in it, with sheets and a blanket and pillows and a bedspread, just like the ones I'd seen on television. And there was a chest of drawers, and a table with more small drawers in it, and two chairs and a mirror and one door that went into a closet and one that led to the bathroom. The fixtures in there were a little different from the ones they'd made for me to practice in, but functionally they seemed about the same.

I didn't look for any difficulty with anything there except the bed, and that wasn't *her* fault, so I assured her everything was just fine, and let her show me how to operate the gas-burner that was set in the wall for heat. Then we went out, and she very carefully locked the door, and handed me the key.

"You better keep that door locked," she said, just a little sharply. "You never know...."

I wanted to ask her *what* you never know, but had the impression that it was something *every*body was supposed to know, so I just nodded and agreed instead.

"You want to get some lunch," she said then, "there's a place down the road isn't too bad. Clean, anyhow, and they don't cater too much to those ... well, it's clean." She pointed the way; you could see the sign from where we were standing. I thanked her, and started the car, and decided I might as well go there as anyplace else, especially since I could see she was watching to find out whether I did or not.

*

These people are all too big. Or almost all of them. But the man behind the counter at the diner was enormous. He was tall and fat with a beefy red face and large open pores and a fleshy mound of a nose. I didn't like to look at him, and when he talked, he boomed so loud I could hardly understand him. On top of all that, the smell in that place was awful: not quite as bad as the drugstore, but some ways similar to it. I kept my eyes on the menu, which was full of unfamiliar words, and tried to remember that I was hungry.

The man was shouting at me—or it was more like growling, I guess—and I couldn't make out the words at first. He said it again, and I sorted out syllables and matched them with the words on the card, and then I got it:

"Goulash is nice today, miss...."

I didn't know what goulash was, and the state my stomach was in, with the smells, I decided I'd better play safe, and ordered a glass of milk, and some vegetable soup.

The milk had a strange taste to it. Not *bad*—just *different*. But of course, this came from cows. That was all right. But the vegetable soup...!

It was quite literally putrid, made as near as I could figure out from dead animal juices, in which vegetables had been soaked and cooked till any trace of flavor or nourishment was entirely removed. I took one taste of that, and then I realized what the really nauseating part of the odor was, in the diner and the drugstore both. It was rotten meat, dead for some time, and then heated in preparation for eating.

The crackers that came with the soup were good; they had a nice salty tang. I ordered more of those, with another glass of milk, and sat back sipping slowly, trying to adjust to that smell, now that I realized I'd probably find it anywhere I could find food.

After a while, I got my insides enough in order so that I could look around a little and see the place, and the other people in it. That was when I turned around and saw Larry sitting next to me.

He was beautiful. He *is* beautiful. I know that's not what you're supposed to say about a man, and he wouldn't like it, but I can only say what I see, and of course that's partly a matter of my own training and my own feelings about myself.

At home on the ship, I always wanted to cut off my hair, because it was so black, and my skin was so white, and they didn't go together. But they wouldn't let me; they liked it that way, I guess, but *I* didn't. No child wants to feel like a freak, and nobody else had hair like that, or dead-white colorless skin, either.

Then, when I went down there, and saw all the humans, I was still a freak because I was so small.

Larry's small, too. Almost as small as I am. And he's all one color. He has hair, of course, but it's so light, and his skin is so dark (both from the sun, I found out), that he looks just about the same lovely golden color all over. Or at least as much of him as showed when I saw him that time, in the diner.

He was beautiful, and he was my size, and he didn't have ugly rough skin or big heavy hands. I stared at him, and I felt like grabbing on to him to make sure he didn't get away.

After a while I realized my mouth was half-open, and I was still holding a cracker, and I remembered that this was very bad manners. I put the cracker down and closed my mouth. He smiled. I didn't know if he was laughing at the odd way I was acting, or just being friendly, but I smiled back anyhow.

"I'm sorry," he said. "I mean, hello. How do you do, and I'm sorry if I startled you. I shouldn't have been staring."

"*You,*" I said, and meant to finish, *You were staring?* But he went right on talking, so that I couldn't finish.

"I don't know what else you can expect, if you go around looking like that," he said.

"I'm sorry...." I started again.

"And you should be," he said sternly. "Anybody who walks into a place like this in the middle of a day like this looking the way you do has got to expect to get stared at a little."

The thing is, I wasn't used to the language; not used *enough*. I could communicate all right, and even understand some jokes, and I knew the spoken language, not some formal unusable version, because I learned it mostly watching those shows on the television screen. But I got confused this time, because "looking" means two different things, active and passive, and I was thinking about how I'd been *looking at* him, and....

That was my lucky day. I didn't want him to be angry at me, and the way I saw it, he was perfectly justified in scolding me, which is what I thought he was doing. But I *knew* he wasn't really angry; I'd have felt it if he was. So I said, "You're right. It was very rude of me, and I don't blame you for being annoyed. I won't do it any more."

He started laughing, and this time I knew it was friendly. Like I said, that was my lucky day; *he* thought I was being witty. And, from what he's told me since, I guess he realized then that *I* felt friendly too, because before that he'd just been bluffing it out, not knowing how to get to know me, and afraid *I'd* be sore at *him*, just for talking to me!

Which goes to show that sometimes you're better off not being *too* familiar with the local customs.

*

The trouble was there were too many things I didn't know, too many small ways to trip myself up. Things they couldn't have foreseen, or if they did, couldn't have done much about. All it took was a little caution and a lot of alertness, plus one big important item: staying in the background—not getting to know any one person too well—not giving any single individual a chance to observe too much about me.

But Larry didn't mean to let me do that. And ... I didn't want him to.

He asked questions; I tried to answer them. I did know enough at least of the conventions to realize that I didn't have to give detailed answers, or could, at any point, act offended at being questioned so much. I *didn't* know enough to realize that reluctance or irritation on my part wouldn't have made him go away. We sat on those stools at the diner for most of an hour, talking, and after a little while I found I could keep the conversation on safer ground by asking *him* about himself, and about the country thereabouts. He seemed to enjoy talking.

Eventually, he had to go back to work. As near as I could make out, he was a test-pilot, or something like it, for a small experimental aircraft plant near the city. He lived not too far from where I was staying, and he wanted to see me that evening.

I hadn't told him where the motel was, and I had at least enough caution left not to tell him, even then. I did agree to meet him at the diner, but for lunch the next day again, instead of that evening. For one thing, I had a lot to do; and for another, I'd seen enough on television shows to know that an evening date was likely to be pretty long-drawn-out, and I wasn't sure I could stand up under that much close scrutiny. I had some studying-up to do first. But the lunch-date was fine; the thought of not seeing him at all was terrifying—as if he were an old friend in a world full of strangers. That was how I felt, that first time, maybe just because he was almost as small as I. But I think it was more than that, really.

*

I drove downtown again, and found a store that seemed to sell all kinds of clothing for women. Then when I got inside, I didn't know where to start, or what to get. I thought of just buying one of everything, so as to fill up a suitcase; the things I had on seemed to be perfectly satisfactory for actual *wearing* purposes. They were quite remarkably—when you stopped to think of it—similar to what most of the women I'd seen that day were wearing, and of course they weren't subject to the same problems of dirtying and wrinkling and such as the clothes in the store were.

I walked around for a while, trying to figure out what all the different items, shapes, sizes, and colors, were for. Some racks and counters had signs, but most of them were unfamiliar words like *brunchies*, or *Bermudas* or *scuffs*; or else they seemed to be mislabeled, like *dusters* for a sort of button-down dress, and *Postage Stamp Girdles* at one section of a long counter devoted to "Foundation Garments." For half an hour or so, I wandered around in there, shaking my head every time a saleswoman came up to me, because I didn't know, and couldn't figure out, what to ask for, or how to ask for it.

The thing was, I didn't dare draw too much attention to myself by doing or saying the wrong things. I'd have to find out more about clothes, somehow, before I could do much buying.

I went out, and on the same block I found a show-window full of suitcases. That was easy. I went in and pointed to one I liked, and paid for it, and walked out with it, feeling a little braver. After all, nobody had to know there was nothing in it. On the corner, I saw some books displayed in the window of a drug store. It took all the courage I had to go in there, after my first trip into one that looked very much like it, but I wanted a dictionary. This place didn't smell quite so strong; I suppose the pharmacy was enclosed in back, and I don't believe it had a lunch counter. Anyhow, I got in and out quickly, and walked back to the car, and sat down with the dictionary.

It turned out to be entirely useless, at least as far as *brunchies* and *Bermudas* were concerned. It had "scuff, v.," with a definition; "v.," I found out, meant *verb*, so that wasn't the word I wanted, but when I remembered the slippers on the counter with the sign, it made sense in a way.

Not enough sense, though. I decided to forget about the clothes for a while. The next problem was a driver's license.

The policeman that morning had been helpful, if over-interested, and since policemen directed traffic, they ought to have the information I wanted. I found one of them standing on a streetcorner looking not too busy, and asked him, and if his hair hadn't been brown instead of reddish (and only half there) I'd have thought it was the same one I talked to before. He wanted to know how old I was, and where was I from, and what I was doing there, and did I have a car, and was I *sure* I was nineteen?

Well, of course, I wasn't sure, but they'd told me that by the local reckoning, that was my approximate age. And I almost slipped and said I *had* a car, until I realized that I didn't have a right to drive one till I had a license. After he asked that one question, I began to feel suspicious about everything else he asked, and the interest he expressed. He was helpful, but I had to remember too, that it was the police who were charged with watching for suspicious characters, and—well, it was the last time I asked a policeman for information.

# EXILE FROM SPACE

He *did* tell me where I could rent a car to take my road test, though, and where to apply for the test. The Courthouse turned out to be the big building behind the square where I'd parked the car that morning, and arranging for the test turned out to be much simpler than, by then, I expected it to be. In a way, I suppose, all the questions I had to answer when I talked to the policeman had prepared me for the official session—though they didn't seem nearly so inquisitive there.

By this time, I'd come to expect that they wouldn't believe my age when I told them. The woman at the window behind the counter wanted to see a "birth certificate," and I produced the one piece of identification I had; an ancient and yellowed document they had kept for me all these years. From the information it contained, I suspected it might even *be* a birth certificate; whether or not, it apparently satisfied her, and after that all she wanted was things like my address and height and weight. Fortunately, they had taken the trouble, back on the ship, to determine these statistics for me, because things like that were always coming up on television shows, especially when people were being questioned by the police. For the address, of course, I used the motel. The rest I knew, and I guess we had the figures close enough to right so that at least the woman didn't question any of it.

I had my road test about half an hour later, in a rented car, and the examiner said I did very well. He seemed surprised, and I don't wonder, considering the way most of those people contrive to mismanage a simple mechanism like an automobile. I guess when they say Earth is still in the Mechanical Age, what they mean is that humans are just *learning* about machines.

*

The biggest single stroke of luck I had at any time came during that road test. We passed a public-looking building with a sign in front that I didn't understand.

"What's that place?" I asked the examiner, and he said, as if anyone would know what he meant, "That? Oh—the Library."

I looked it up in my dictionary as soon as I was done at the License Bureau, and when I found out what it was, everything became a great deal simpler.

18

There was a woman who worked there, who showed me, without any surprise at my ignorance, just how the card catalogue worked, and what the numbering system meant; she didn't ask me how old I was, or any other questions, or demand any proof of any kind to convince her I had a right to use the place. She didn't even bother me much with questions about what I was looking for. I told her there were a *lot* of things I wanted to know, and she seemed to think that was a good answer, and said if she could help me any way, not to hesitate to ask, and then she left me alone with those drawers and drawers full of letter-and-number keys to all the mysteries of an alien world.

I found a book on how to outfit your daughter for college, that started with underwear and worked its way through to jewelry and cosmetics. I also found a whole shelf full of law books, and in one of them, specific information about the motor vehicle regulations in different States. There was a wonderful book about diamonds and other precious stones, particularly fascinating because it went into the chemistry of the different stones, and gave me the best measuring-stick I found at any time to judge the general level of technology of that so-called Mechanical Age.

That was all I had time for, I couldn't believe it was so late, when the librarian came and told me they were closing up, and I guess my disappointment must have showed all over me, because she asked if I wouldn't like to have a card, so I could take books home?

I found out all I needed to get a card was identification. I was supposed to have a reference, too, but the woman said she thought perhaps it would be all right without one, in my case. And then, when I wanted to take a volume of the Encyclopedia Americana, she said they didn't usually circulate that, but if I thought I could bring it back within a day or two....

I promised to, and I never did, and out of everything that happened, that's the one thing I feel badly about. I think she must have been a very unusual and *good* sort of woman, and I wish I had kept my promise to her.

*

Some of the stores downtown were still open. I bought the things I'd be expected to have, as near as I could make out from the book on college girls: panties and a garter belt and a brassiere, and stockings. A slip and another blouse, and a coat, because even in the early evening it was beginning to get chilly. Then the salesgirl talked me into gloves and a scarf and some earrings. I was halfway back to the car when I remembered about night clothes, and went back for a gown and robe and slippers. That didn't begin to complete the college girls' list, but it seemed like a good start. I'd need a dress, too, I thought, if I ever did go out with Larry in the evening ... but that could wait.

I put everything into the suitcase, and drove back to the motel. On the way, I stopped at a food store, and bought a large container of milk, and some crackers, and some fruit—oranges and bananas and apples. Back in my room, I put everything away in the drawers, and then sat down with my book and my food, and had a wonderful time. I was hungry, and everything tasted good, away from the dead meat smells, and what with clothes in the drawers and everything, I was beginning to feel like a real Earth-girl.

I even took a bath in the bathroom.

A good long one. Next to the library, that's the thing I miss most. It would be even better, if they made the tubs bigger, so you could swim around some. But just getting wet all over like that, and splashing in the water, is fun. Of course, we could never spare enough water for that on the ship.

Altogether, it was a good evening; everything was fine until I tried to sleep in that bed. I felt as if I was being suffocated all over. The floor was almost as bad, but in a different way. And once I got to sleep, I guess I slept well enough, because I felt fine in the morning. But then, I think I must have been on a mild oxygen jag all the time I was down there; nothing seemed to bother me too much. That morning, I felt so good I worked up my courage to go into a restaurant again—a different one. The smell was beginning to be familiar, and I could manage better. I experimented with a cereal called oatmeal, which was delicious, then I went back to the motel, packed up all my new belongings, left the key on the desk—as instructed by the sign on the door—and started out for Denver.

*

Denver, according to the Encyclopedia Americana, is more of a true metropolitan area than Colorado Springs; that means—on Earth—that it is dirtier, more crowded, far less pleasant to look at or live in, and a great deal more convenient and efficient to do business in. In Denver, and with the aid of a Colorado driver's license for casual identification, I was able to sell two of my larger diamonds fairly quickly, at two different places, for something approximating half of their full value. Then I parked the car they had given me on a side street, took my suitcase, coat, and book with me, and walked to the nearest car sales lot. I left the keys in the old car, for the convenience of anyone who might want it.

Everything went extraordinarily smoothly, with just one exception. I had found out everything I needed to know in that library, except that when dealing with humans, one must always allow for waste time. If I had realized that at the time I left Colorado Springs that morning, everything might have turned out very differently indeed—although when I try to think just what other way it *could* have turned out, I don't quite know ... and I wonder, too, how much they knew, or planned, before they sent me down there....

This much is sure: if I hadn't assumed that a 70-mile trip, with a 60-mile average speed limit, would take approximately an hour and a half, and if I had realized that buying an automobile was not the same simple process as buying a nightgown, I wouldn't have been late for my luncheon appointment. And if I'd been there on time, I'd never have made the date for that night. As it was, I started out at seven o'clock in the morning, and only by exceeding the speed limit on the last twenty miles of the return trip did I manage to pull into that diner parking space at five minutes before two.

His car was still there!

It is so easy to look back and spot the instant of recognition or of error. My relief when I saw his car ... my delight when I walked in and saw and *felt* his mixture of surprise and joy that I had come, with disappointment and frustration because it was so late, and he had to leave almost immediately. And my complete failure, in the midst of the complexities of these inter-reactions, to think logically, or to recognize that his ordinary perceptions were certainly the equivalent of my own....

At that moment, I wasn't thinking *about* any of these things. I spent a delirious sort of five minute period absorbing his feelings about me, and releasing my own at him. I hadn't planned to do it, not so soon, not till I knew much more than I did—perhaps after another week's reading and going about—but when he said that since I'd got there so late for lunch, I'd *have* to meet him for dinner, I found I agreed with him perfectly.

*

That afternoon, I bought a dress. This, too, took a great deal of time, even more than the car, because in the one case I simply had to look at a number of component parts, and listen to the operation of the motor, and feel for the total response of the mechanism, to determine whether it was suitable or not—but in the other, I had nothing to guide me but my own untrained taste, and the dubious preferences of the salesgirl, plus what I *thought* Larry's reactions *might* be. Also, I had to determine, without seeming too ignorant, just what sort of dress might be suitable for a dinner date—and without knowing for sure just how elaborate Larry's plans for the evening might be.

I learned a lot, and was startled to find that I enjoyed myself tremendously. But I couldn't make up my mind, and bought three dresses instead of one. It was after that, emboldened by pleasure and success, that I went back to that first drugstore. The Encyclopedia volume I had taken from the library, besides containing the information I wanted on Colorado, had an article on Cosmetics. I decided powder was unnecessary, although I could understand easily enough how important it must be to the native women, with their thick skin and large pores and patchy coloring; that accounted for the fact that the men were mostly so much uglier ... and I wondered if Larry used it, and if that was why his skin looked so much better than the others'.

Most of the perfumes made me literally ill; a few were inoffensive or mildly pleasant, if you thought of them just as smells, and not as something to be mistaken for one's *own* smell. Apparently, though, from the amount of space given over to them on the counter, and the number of advertisements I had seen or heard for one brand or another, they were an essential item. I picked out a faint lavender scent, and then bought some lipstick, mascara, and eyebrow pencil. On these last purchases, it was a relief to find that I had no opportunity to display my ignorance about nuances of coloring, or the merits of one brand over another. The woman behind the counter knew exactly what I should have, and was not interested in hearing any of my opinions. She even told me how to apply the mascara, which was helpful, since the other two were obvious, and anyhow I'd seen them used on television, and the lipstick especially I had seen women use since I'd been here.

It turned out to be a little more difficult than it looked, when I tried it. Cosmetics apparently take a good deal more experience than clothing, if you want to have it look *right*. Right by *their* standards, I mean, so that your face becomes a formal design, and will register only a minimum of actual emotion or response.

I was supposed to meet Larry in the cocktail lounge of a hotel in Manitou Springs, the smaller town I'd passed through the day before on my way down from the mountain. I drove back that way now, with all my possessions in my new car, including the purse that held not only my remaining diamonds and birth certificate, but also a car registration, driver's license, wallet, money, and makeup. A little more than halfway there, I saw a motel with a "Vacancy" sign out, and an attractive clean look about it. I pulled in and got myself a room with no more concern than if I'd been doing that sort of thing all my life.

This time there was no question about my age, nor was there later on that evening, in the cocktail lounge or anywhere else. I suppose it was the lipstick that made the difference, plus a certain increase in self-confidence; apparently I wasn't too small to be an adult, provided I looked and acted like one.

The new room did not have a bathtub. There was a shower, which was fun, but not as much as the tub had been. Dressing was *not* fun, and when I was finished, the whole effect still didn't look right, in terms of my own mental image of an Earth-woman dressed for a date.

It was the shoes, of course. This kind of dress wanted high heels. I had tried a pair in the store, and promptly rejected the whole notion. Now I wondered if I'd been too hasty, but I realized I could not conceivably have added that discomfort to the already-pressing difficulties of stockings and garter belt.

This last problem got so acute when I sat down and tried to drive the car, that I did some thinking about it, and decided to take them off. It seemed to me that I'd seen a lot of bare legs with flat heels. It was only with high heels that stockings were a real necessity. Anyhow, I pulled the car over to the side on an empty stretch of road, and wriggled out of things with a great deal of difficulty. I don't believe it made much difference in my appearance. No one *seemed* to notice, and I do think the lack of heels was more important.

*

All of this has been easy to put down. The next part is harder: partly because it's so important; partly because it's personal; partly because I just don't remember it all as clearly.

Larry was waiting for me when I got to the hotel. He stood up and walked over to me, looking at me as if I were the only person in the room besides himself, or as if he'd been waiting all his life, and only just that moment saw what it was he'd been waiting for. I don't know how I looked at him, but I know how I felt all of a sudden, and I don't think I can express it very well.

It was odd, because of the barriers to communication. The way he felt and the way I did are not things to put into words, and although I couldn't help but feel the impact of *his* emotion, I had to remember that he was deaf-and-blind to mine. All I could get from him for that matter, was a sort of generalized *noise*, loud but confused, without any features or details.

He smiled, and I smiled, and he said, "I didn't know if you'd really come ..." and I said, "Am I late?" and he said, "Not much. What do you want to drink?"

I knew he meant something with alcohol in it, and I didn't dare, not till I'd experimented all alone first.

"Could I get some orange juice?" I asked.

He smiled again. "You can get anything you want. You don't drink?" He took my arm, and walked me over to a booth in the back corner, and went on without giving me a chance to answer. "No, of course you don't. Just orange juice and milk. Listen, Tina, I've been scared to ask you, but we might as well get it over with. How old are you anyhow?..." We sat down, but he still didn't give me a chance to answer. "No, that's not the right question. Who are you? What are you? What makes a girl like you exist at all? How come they let you run around on your own like this? Does your mother.... Never mind me, honey. I've got no business asking anything. Sufficient unto the moment, and all that. I'm just talking so much because I'm so nervous. I haven't felt like this since ... since I first went up for a solo in a Piper Cub. I didn't think you'd come, and you did, and you're still here in spite of me and my dumb yap. Orange juice for the lady, please," he told the waiter, "and a beer for me. Draft."

I just sat there. As long as he kept talking, I didn't have to. He looked just as beautiful as he had in the diner, only maybe more so. His skin was smoother; I suppose he'd just shaved. And he was wearing a tan suit just a shade darker than his skin, which was just a shade darker than his hair, and there was absolutely nothing I could say out loud in his language that would mean anything at all, so I waited to see if he'd start talking again.

"You're not mad at me, Tina?"

I smiled and shook my head.

"Well, *say* something then."

"It's more fun listening to you."

"You say that just like you mean it ... or do you mean *funny*?"

"No. I mean that it's hard for me to talk much. I don't know how to say a lot of the things I want to say. And most people don't say anything when they talk, and I don't like listening to their voices, but I do like yours, and ... I can't help liking what you say ... it's always so *nice*. About me, I mean. Complimentary. Flattering."

"You were right the first time. And you seem to be able to say what you mean very clearly."

Which was just the trouble. Not only able to, but unable not to. It didn't take any special planning or remembering to say or act the necessary lies to other humans. But Larry was the least alien person I'd ever known. Dishonesty to him was like lying to myself. Playing a role for him was pure schizophrenia.

Right then, I knew it was a mistake. I should never have made that date, or at least not nearly so soon. But even as I thought that, I had no more intention of cutting it short or backing out than I did of going back to the ship the next day. I just tried not to talk too much, and trusted to the certain knowledge that I was as important to him as he was to me—so perhaps whatever mistakes I made, whatever I said that sounded *wrong*, he would either accept or ignore or forgive.

But of course you can't just sit all night and say nothing. And the simplest things could trip me up. Like when he asked if I'd like to dance, and all I had to say was "No, thanks," and instead, because I *wanted* to try it, I said, "I don't know how."

Or when he said something about going to a movie, and I agreed enthusiastically, and he gave me a choice of three different ones that he wanted to see ... "Oh, anyone," I told him. "You're easy to please," he said, but he insisted on my making a choice. There was something he called "an old-Astaire-Rogers," and something else that was made in England, and one current American one with stars I'd seen on television. I wanted to see either of the others. I could have said so, or I could have named one, any one. Instead I heard myself blurting out that I'd never been to a movie.

At that point, of course, he began to ask questions in earnest. And at that point, schizoid or not, I had to lie. It was easier, though, because I'd been thoroughly briefed in my story, for just such emergencies as this—and because I could talk more or less uninterruptedly, with only pertinent questions thrown in, and without having to react so much to the emotional tensions between us.

I told him how my parents had died in an automobile accident when I was a baby; how my two uncles had claimed me at the hospital; about the old house up on the mountainside, and the convent school, and the two old men who hated the evils of the world; about the death of the first uncle, and at long last the death of the second, and the lawyers and the will and everything—the whole story, as we'd worked it out back on the ship.

It answered everything, explained everything—even the unexpected item of not being able to eat meat. My uncles were vegetarians, which was certainly a harmless eccentricity compared to most of the others I credited them with.

As a story, it was pretty far-fetched, but it hung together—and in certain ways, it wasn't even *too* far removed from the truth. It was, anyhow, the closest thing to the truth that I could tell—and I therefore delivered it with a fair degree of conviction. Of course it wasn't designed to stand up to the close and personal inspection Larry gave it; but then he *wanted* to believe me.

He seemed to swallow it. What he did, of course, was something any man who relies, as he did, on his reflexes and responses to stay alive, learns to do very early—he filed all questions and apparent discrepancies for reference, or for thinking over when there was time, and proceeded to make the most of the current situation.

We both made the most of it. It was a wonderful evening, from that point on. We went to the Astaire-Rogers picture, and although I missed a lot of the humor, since it was contemporary stuff from a time before I had any chance to learn about Earth, the music and dancing were fun. Later on, I found that dancing was not nearly as difficult or intricate as it looked—at least not with Larry. All I had to do was give in to a natural impulse to let my body follow his. It felt wonderful, from the feet on up.

Finally, we went back to the hotel, where we'd left my car, and I started to get out of his, but he reached out an arm, and stopped me.

"There's something else I guess you never did," he said. His voice sounded different from before. He put both his hands on my shoulders, and pulled me toward him, and leaned over and kissed me.

I'd seen it, of course, on television.

I'd seen it, but I had no idea....

That first time, it was something I felt on my lips, and felt so sweetly and so strongly that the rest of me seemed to melt away entirely. I had no other sensations, except in that one place where his mouth touched mine. That was the first time.

When it stopped, the world stopped, and I began again, but I had to sort out the parts and pieces and put them all together to find out who I was. While I did this, his hands were still on my shoulders, where they'd been all along, only he was holding me at arm's distance away from him, and looking at me curiously.

"It really was, wasn't it?" he said.

"What?" I tried to say, but the sound didn't come out. I took a breath and "Was what?" I croaked.

"The first time." He smiled suddenly, and it was like the sun coming up in the morning, and then his arms went all the way around me. I don't know whether he moved over on the seat, or I did, or both of us. "Oh, baby, baby," he whispered in my ear, and then there was the second time.

The second time was like the first, and also like dancing, and some ways like the bathtub. This time none of me melted away; it was all there, and all close to him, and all warm, and all tingling with sensations. I was more completely alive right then than I had ever been before in my life.

# EXILE FROM SPACE

After we stopped kissing each other, we stayed very still, holding on to each other, for a while, and then he moved away just a little, enough, to breathe better.

I didn't know what to do. I didn't want to get out of the car. I didn't even want to be separated from him by the two or three inches between us on the seat. But he was sitting next to me now, staring straight ahead, not saying anything, and I just didn't know what came next. On television, the kiss was always the end of the scene.

He started the car again.

I said, "I have to ... my car ... I...."

"We'll come back," he said. "Don't worry about it. We'll come back. Let's just drive a little...?" he pulled out past my car, and turned and looked at me for a minute. "You don't want to go now, do you? Right away?"

I shook my head, but he wasn't looking at me any more, so I took a breath and said out loud, "No."

We came off a twisty street onto the highway. "So that's how it hits you," he said. He wasn't exactly talking to me; more like thinking out loud. "Twenty-seven years a cool cat, and now it has to be a crazy little midget that gets to you." He had to stop then, for a red light—the same light I'd stopped at the first time on the way in. That seemed a long long time before.

Larry turned around and took my hand. He looked hard at my face, "I'm sorry, hon. I didn't mean that the way it sounded."

"What?" I said. "What do you mean?" I hadn't even tried to make sense out of what he was saying before; he wasn't talking to me anyhow.

"Kid," he said, "maybe that was the first time for you, but in a different way it was the first time for me too." His hand opened and closed around mine, and his mouth opened and closed too, but nothing came out. The light was green; he noticed, and started moving, but it turned red again. This time he kept watching it.

"I don't suppose anybody ever told you about the birds and the bees and the butterflies," he said.

"Told me *what* about them?" He didn't answer right away, so I thought about it. "All I can think of is they all have wings. They all fly."

"So do I. So does a fly. What I mean is ... the hell with it!" He turned off the highway, and we went up a short hill and through a sort of gateway between two enormous rocks. "Have you ever been here?" he asked.

"I don't think so...."

"They call it The Garden of the Gods. I don't know why. I like it here ... it's a good place to drive and think."

There was a lot of moonlight, and the Garden was all hills and drops and winding roads between low-growing brush, and everywhere, as if the creatures of some giant planet had dropped them, were those towering rocks, their shapes scooped out and chiseled and hollowed and twisted by wind, water and sand. Yes, it was lovely, and it was non-intrusive. Just what he said—a good place to drive and think.

Once he came to the top of a hill, and stopped the car, and we looked out over the Garden, spreading out in every direction, with the moonlight shadowed in the sagebrush, and gleaming off the great rocks. Then we turned and looked at each other, and he reached out for me and kissed me again; after which he pulled away as if the touch of me hurt him, and grabbed hold of the wheel with a savage look on his face, and raced the motor, and raised a cloud of dust on the road behind us.

I didn't understand, and I felt hurt. I wanted to stop again. I wanted to be kissed again. I didn't like sitting alone on my side of the seat, with that growl in his throat not quite coming out.

I asked him to stop again. He shook his head, and made believe to smile.

"I'll buy you a book," he said. "All about the birds and the bees and a little thing we have around here we call sex. I'll buy it tomorrow, and you can read it—you *do* know how to read, don't you?—and then we'll take another ride, and we can park if you want to. Not tonight, baby."

"But I *know*...." I started, and then had sense enough to stop. I knew about sex; but what I knew about it didn't connect with kissing or parking the car, or sitting close ... and it occurred to me that maybe it did, and maybe there was a lot I *didn't* know that wasn't on Television, and wasn't on the Ship's reference tapes either. Morals and mores, and nuances of behavior. So I shut up, and let him take me back to the hotel again, to my own car.

He leaned past me to open the door on my side, but he couldn't quite make it, and I had my fourth kiss. Then he let go again, and almost pushed me out of the car; but when I started to close the door behind me, he called out, "Tomorrow night?"

"I ... all right," I said. "Yes. Tomorrow night."

"Can I pick you up?"

There was no reason not to this time. The first time I wouldn't tell him where I lived, because I knew I'd have to change places, and I didn't know where yet. I told him the name of the motel, and where it was.

"Six o'clock," he said.

"All right."

"Good night."

"Good night."

*

I don't remember driving back to my room. I think I slept on the bed that night, without ever stopping to determine whether it was comfortable or not. And when I woke up in the morning, and looked out the window at a white-coated landscape, the miracle of snow (which I had never seen before; not many planets have as much water vapor in their atmospheres as Earth does.) in summer weather seemed trivial in comparison to what had happened to me.

Trivial, but beautiful. I was afraid it would be very cold, but it wasn't.

I had gathered, from the weather-talk in the place where I ate breakfast, that in this mountain-country (it was considered to be very high altitude there), snow at night and hot sun in the afternoon was not infrequent in the month of April, though it was unusual for May.

It was beautiful to look at, and nice to walk on, but it began melting as soon as the sun was properly up, and then it looked awful. The red dirt there is pretty, and so is the snow, but when they began merging into each other in patches and muddy spots, it was downright ugly.

Not that I cared. I ate oatmeal and drank milk and nibbled at a piece of toast, and tried to plan my activities for the day. To the library first, and take back the book they'd lent me. Book ... all right then, get a book on sex. But that was foolish; I *knew* all about sex. At least I knew ... well, what did I know? I knew their manner of reproduction, and....

Just why, at that time and place, I should have let it come through to me, I don't know. I'd managed to stay in a golden daze from the time in

30

the Garden till that moment, refusing to think through the implications of what Larry said.

Sex. Sex is mating and reproduction. Dating and dancing and kissing are parts of the courtship procedure. And the television shows all stop with kissing, because the mating itself is taboo. Very simple. Also *very* taboo.

Of course, they didn't *say* I couldn't. They never said anything about it at all. It was just obvious. It wouldn't even work. We were *different*, after all.

Oh, technically, biologically, of course, we were probably cross-fertile, but....

The whole thing was so obviously *impossible*!

They should have warned me. I'd never have let it go this far, if I'd known.

Sex. Mating. Marriage. Tribal rites. Rituals and rigamaroles, and stay here forever. Never go back.

*Never go back?*

There was an instant's sheer terror, and then the comforting knowledge that they wouldn't *let* me do that. I had to go back.

Baby on a spaceship?

Well, *I* was a baby on a spaceship, but that was different. How different? I was older. I wasn't born there. Getting born is complicated. Oxygen, gravity, things like that. You can't raise a *human* baby on a spaceship.... *Human?* What's human? What am I? Never mind the labels. It would be *my* baby....

I didn't want a baby. I just wanted Larry to hold me close to him and kiss me.

*

I drove downtown and on the way to the library I passed a bookstore, so I stopped and went in there instead. That was better. I could buy what I wanted, and not have to ask permission to take it out, and if there was more than one, I could have all I wanted.

I asked the man for books about sex. He looked so startled, I realized the taboo must apply on the verbal level too.

I didn't care. He showed me where the books were, and that's all that mattered. "Non-fiction here," he said. "That what you wanted, Miss?"

31

# EXILE FROM SPACE

Non-fiction. Definitely. I thanked him, and picked out half a dozen different books. One was a survey of sexual behavior and morals; another was a manual of techniques; one was on the psychology of sex, and there was another about abnormal sex, and one on physiology, and just to play safe, considering the state of my own ignorance, one that announced itself as giving a "clear simple explanation of the facts of life for adolescents."

I took them all to the counter, and paid for them, and the man still looked startled, but he took the money. He insisted on wrapping them up, though, before I could leave.

*

The next part of this is really Larry's story, but unable as I am, even now, to be *certain* about his unspoken thoughts, I can only tell it as I experienced it. I didn't do anything all that day, except wade through the books I'd bought, piece-meal, reading a few pages here and a chapter there. The more I read, the more confused I got. Each writer contradicted all the others, except in regard to the few basic biological facts that I already knew. The only real addition to my factual knowledge was the information in the manual of technique about contraception—and that was rather shocking, even while it was tempting.

The mechanical contrivances these people made use of were foolish, of course, and typical of the stage of culture they are going through. If I wanted to prevent conception, while engaging in an act of sexual intercourse, I could, do so, of course, but....

The shock to the glandular system wouldn't be too severe; it was the psychological repercussions I was thinking about. The idea of pursuing a course of action whose sole motivation was the procreative urge, and simultaneously to decide by an act of will to refuse to procreate....

I *could* do it, theoretically, but in practice I knew I never would.

I put the book down and went outside in the afternoon sunshine. The motel was run by a young married couple, and I watched the woman come out and put her baby in the playpen. She was laughing and talking to it; she looked happy; so did the baby.

But I wouldn't be. Not even if they let me. I couldn't live here and bring up a child—children?—on this primitive, almost barbaric, world. Never ever be able fully to communicate with anyone. Never, ever, be entirely honest with anyone.

32

Then I remembered what it was like to be in Larry's arms, and wondered what kind of communication I could want that might surpass that. Then I went inside and took a shower and began to dress for the evening.

It was too early to get dressed. I was ready too soon. I went out and got in the car, and pulled out onto the highway and started driving. I was halfway up the mountain before I knew where I was going, and then I doubled my speed.

I was scared. I ran away.

*

There was still some snow on the mountain top. Down below, it would be warm yet, but up there it was cold. The big empty house was full of dust and chill and I brought fear in with me. I wished I had known where I was going when I left my room; I wanted my coat. I wanted something to read while I waited. I remembered the library book and almost went back. Instead, I went to the dark room in back that had once been somebody's kitchen, and opened the cupboard and found the projector and yelled for help.

I didn't know where they were, how far away, whether cruising or landed somewhere, or how long it would take. All I could be sure of was that they couldn't come till after dark, full dark, and that would be, on the mountain top, at least another four hours.

There was a big round black stove in a front room, that looked as if it could burn wood safely. I went out and gathered up everything I could find nearby that looked to be combustible, and started a fire, and began to feel better. I beat the dust off a big soft chair, and pulled it over close to the stove, and curled up in it, warm and drowsy and knowing that help was on the way.

I fell asleep, and I was in the car with Larry again, in front of that hotel, every cell of my body tinglingly awake, and I woke up, and moved the chair farther back away from the fire, and watched the sun set through the window—till I fell asleep again, and dreamed again, and when I woke, the sun was gone, but the mountain top was brightly lit. I had forgotten about the moon.

I tried to remember what time it rose and when it set, but all I knew was it had shone as bright last night in the Garden of the Gods.

I walked around, and went outside, and got more wood, and when it was hot in the room again, I fell asleep, and Larry's hands were on my shoulders, but he wasn't kissing me.

He was shouting at me. He sounded furious, but I couldn't feel any anger. "You God-damn little idiot!" he shouted. "What in the name of all that's holy...? ... put you over my knee and.... For God's sake, baby," he stopped shouting, "what did you pull a dumb trick like this for?"

"I was scared. I didn't even plan to do it. I just did."

"Scared? My God, I should think you would be! Now listen, babe. I don't know yet what's going on, and I don't think I'm going to like it when I find out. I don't like it already that you told me a pack of lies last night. Just the same, God help me, I don't think it's what it sounds like. But I'm the only one who doesn't. Now you better give it to me straight, because they've got half the security personnel of this entire area out hunting for you, and nobody else is going to care much what the truth is. My God, on top of everything else, you had to *run away*! Now, give out, kid, and make it good. This one has got to stick."

I didn't understand a lot of what he said. I started trying to explain, but he wouldn't listen. He wanted something else, and I didn't know what.

Finally, he made me understand.

He'd almost believed my story the night before. Almost, but there was a detail somewhere that bothered him. He couldn't remember it at first; it kept nudging around the edge of his mind, but he didn't know what it was. He forgot about it for a while. Then, in the Garden, I made my second big mistake. (He didn't explain all of this then; he just accused, and I didn't understand this part completely until later.) I wanted him to park the car.

Any girl on Earth, no matter how sheltered, how inexperienced, would have known better than that. As he saw it, he had to decide whether I was just so carried away by the night and the mood and the moment that I didn't *care*—or whether my apparent innocence was a pose all along.

When we separated in front of the hotel that night, we both had to take the same road for a while. Larry was driving right behind me for a good three miles, before I turned off at the motel. And that was when he realized what the detail was that had been bothering him: my car.

The first time he saw me, I was driving a different make and model, with Massachusetts plates on it. He was sure of that, because he had copied it down when he left the luncheonette, the first time we met.

Larry had never told me very clearly about the kind of work he did. I knew it was something more or less "classified," having to do with aircraft—jet planes or experimental rockets, or something like that. And I knew, without his telling me, that the work—not just the *job*, but the work he did at it—was more important to him than anything else ever had been. More important, certainly, than he had ever expected any woman to be.

So, naturally, when he met me that day, and knew he wanted to see me again, but couldn't get my address or any other identifying information out of me, he had copied down the license number of my car, and turned it in, with my name, to the Security Officer on the Project. A man who has spent almost every waking moment from the age of nine planning and preparing to fit himself for a role in humanity's first big fling into space doesn't endanger his security status by risking involuntary contamination from an attractive girl. The little aircraft plant on the fringes of town was actually a top-secret key division in the Satellite project, and if you worked there, you took precautions.

The second time I met him at the luncheonette, he had been waiting so long, and had so nearly given up any hope of my coming, that he was no longer watching the road or the door when I finally got there—and when he left, he was so pleased at having gotten a dinner date with me, that he didn't notice much of anything at all. Not except out of the corner of one eye, and with only the slightest edge of subconscious recognition: just enough so that some niggling detail that was out-of-place kept bothering him thereafter; and just enough so that he made a point of stopping in the Security Office again that afternoon to add my new motel address to the information he'd given them the day before.

The three-mile drive in back of my Colorado plates was just about long enough, finally, to make the discrepancy register consciously.

Larry went home and spent a bad night. His feelings toward me, as I could hardly understand at the time, were a great deal stronger, or at least more clearly defined, than mine about him. But since he was more certain just what it was he wanted, and less certain what *I* did, every time he tried to fit my attitude in the car into the rest of what he knew, he'd come up with a different answer, and nine answers out of ten were angry and suspicious and agonizing.

"Now look, babe," he said, "you've got to see this. I trusted *you*; really, all the time, I did trust you. But I didn't trust *me*. By the time I went to work this morning, I was half-nuts. I didn't know *what* to think, that's all. And I finally sold myself on the idea that if you were what you said you were, nobody would get hurt, and—well, if you *weren't* on the level, I better find out, quick. You see that?"

"Yes," I said.

"Okay. So I told them about the license plates, and about—the other stuff."

"What other stuff?" What else was there? How stupid could I be?

"I mean, the—in the car. The way you—Listen, kid," he said, his face grim and demanding again. "It's still just as true as it was then. I *still* don't know. They called me this evening, and said when they got around to the motel to question you, you'd skipped out. They also said that Massachusetts car was stolen. And there were a couple of other things they'd picked up that they wouldn't tell me, but they've got half the National Guard and all the Boy Scouts out after you by now. They wanted me to tell them anything I could think of that might help them find this place. I couldn't think of anything while I was talking to them. Right afterwards, I remembered plenty of things—which roads you were familiar with, and what you'd seen before and what you hadn't, stuff like that, so—"

"So you—?"

"So I came out myself. I wanted to find you first. Listen, babe, I love you. Maybe I'm a sucker, and maybe I'm nuts, and maybe I-don't-know-what. But I figured maybe I could find out more, and easier on you, than they could. And honey, it better be good, because I don't think I've got what it would take to turn you in, and now I've found you—"

He let it go there, but that was plenty. He was willing to listen. He wanted to believe in me, because he wanted me. And finding me in the house I'd described, where I'd said it was, had him half-convinced. But I still had to explain those Massachusetts plates. And I couldn't.

I was psychologically incapable of telling him another lie, now, when I knew I would never see him again, that this was the last time I could ever possibly be close to him in any way. I couldn't estrange myself by lying.

*

And I was *also* psychologically incapable—I found out—of telling the truth. They'd seen to that.

It was the first time I'd ever hated them. The first time, I suppose, that I fully realized my position with them.

I could not tell the truth, and I would not tell a lie; all I could do was explain this, and hope he would believe me. I could explain, too, that I was no spy, no enemy; that those who had prevented me from telling what I wanted to tell were no menace to his government or his people.

He believed me.

It was just that simple. He believed me, because I suppose he knew, without knowing how he knew it, that it was truth. Humans are not incapable of communication; they are simply unaware of it.

I told him, also, that they were coming for me, that I had called them, and—regretfully—that he had better leave before they came.

"You said they weren't enemies or criminals. You were telling the truth, weren't you?"

"Yes, I was. They won't *harm* you. But they might...." I couldn't say it. I didn't know the words when I tried to say it. *Might take you away with them ... with us....*

"Might what?"

"Might ... oh, I don't *know!*"

Now he was suspicious again. "All right," he said. "I'll leave. You come with me."

It was just that simple. Go back with him. Let them come and not find me. What could they do? Their own rules would keep them from hunting for me. They couldn't come down among the people of Earth. Go back. Stop running.

We got into his car, and he turned around and smiled at me again, like the other time.

I smiled back, seeing him through a shiny kind of mist which must have been tears. I reached for him, and he reached for me at the same time.

37

# EXILE FROM SPACE

When we let go, he tried to start the car, and it wouldn't work. Of course. I'd forgotten till then. I started laughing and crying at the same time in a sort of a crazy way, and took him back inside and showed him the projector. They'd forgotten to give me any commands about not doing that, I guess. Or they thought it wouldn't matter.

It did matter. Larry looked it over, and puzzled over it a little, and fooled around, and asked me some questions. I didn't have much technical knowledge, but I knew what it did, and he figured out the way it did it. Nothing with an electro-magnetic motor was going to work while that thing was turned on, not within a mile or so in any direction. And there wasn't any way to turn it off. It was a homing beam, and it was on to stay—foolproof.

That was when he looked at me, and said slowly, "You got here three days ago, didn't you, babe?"

I nodded.

"There was—God-damn it, it's too foolish! There was a—a *flying saucer* story in the paper that day. Somebody saw it land on a hilltop somewhere. Some crackpot. Some ... how about it, kid?"

I couldn't say yes and I couldn't say no, and I did the only thing that was left, which was to get hysterical. In a big way.

He had to calm me down, of course. And I found out why the television shows stop with the kiss. The rest is very private and personal.

*

*Author's note: This story was dictated to me by a five-year-old boy—word-for-word, except for a very few editorial changes of my own. He is a very charming and bright youngster who plays with my own five-year-old daughter. One day he wandered into my office, and watched me typing for a while, then asked what I was doing. I answered (somewhat irritably, because the children are supposed to stay out of the room when I'm working) that I was trying to write a story.*

*"What kind of a story?"*

*"A grown-up story."*

*"But what kind?"*

*"A science-fiction story." The next thing I was going to do was to call my daughter, and ask her to take her company back to the playroom. I had my mouth open, but I never got a syllable out. Teddy was talking.*

*"I don't know where they got the car," he said. "They made three or four stops before the last...." He had a funny look on his face, and his eyes were glazed-looking.*

*I had seen some experimental work with hypnosis and post-hypnotic performance. After the first couple of sentences, I led Teddy into the living-room, and switched on the tape-recorder. I left it on as long as he kept talking. I had to change tapes once, and missed a few more sentences. When he was done, I asked him, with the tape still running, where he had heard that story.*

*"What story?" he asked. He looked perfectly normal again.*

*"The story you just told me."*

*He was obviously puzzled.*

*"The science-fiction story," I said.*

*"I don't know where they got the car," he began; his face was set and his eyes were blank.*

*I kept the tape running, and picked up the parts I'd missed before. Then I sent Teddy off to the playroom, and played back the tape, and thought for a while.*

*There was a little more, besides what you've read. Parts of it were confused, with some strange words mixed in, and with sentences half-completed, and a feeling of ambivalence or censorship or inhibition of some kind preventing much clarity. Other parts were quite clear. Of these, the only section I have omitted so far that seems to me to belong in the story is this one:—*

*

The baby will have to be born on Earth! They have decided that themselves. And for the first time, I am glad that they cannot communicate with me as perfectly as they do among themselves. I can think some things they do not know about.

We are not coming back. I do not think that I will like it on Earth for very long, and I do not know—neither does Larry—what will happen to us when the Security people find us, and we cannot answer their questions. But—

I am a woman now, and I love like a woman. Larry will not be their pet; so I cannot be. I am not sure that I am fit to be what Larry thinks of as a "human being." He says I must learn to be "my own master." I am not at all sure I could do this, if it were necessary, but fortunately, this is one of Larry's areas of semantic confusion. The feminine of *master* is *mistress*, which has various meanings.

39

# EXILE FROM SPACE

Also, there is the distinct possibility, from what Larry says, that we will not, *either* of us, be allowed even as much liberty as we have here.

There is also the matter of gratitude. *They* brought me up, took care of me, taught me, loved me, gave me a way of life, and a knowledge of myself, infinitely richer than I could ever have had on Earth. Perhaps they even saved my life, healing me when I was quite possibly beyond the power of Earthly medical science to save. But against all this—

*They* caused the damage to start with. It was *their* force-field that wrecked the car and killed my parents. *They* have paid for it; *they* are paying for it yet. *They* will continue to pay, for more years than make sense in terms of a human lifetime. *They* will continue to wander from planet to planet and system to system, because *they* have broken *their* own law, and now may never go home.

But *I* can.

I am a woman, and Larry is a man. We will go home and have our baby. And perhaps the baby will be the means of our freedom, some day. If we cannot speak to save ourselves, he may some day be able to speak for us.

I do not think the blocks they set in us will penetrate my womb as my own thoughts, I hope, already have.

*

*Author's note: Before writing this story—as a story—I talked with Johnny's parents. I approached them cautiously. His mother is a big woman, and a brunette. His father is a friendly fat redhead. I already knew that neither of them reads science-fiction. The word is not likely to be mentioned in their household.*

*They moved to town about three years ago. Nobody here knew them before that, but there are rumors that Johnny is adopted. They did not volunteer any confirmation of that information when I talked to them, and they did not pick up on any of the leads I offered about his recitation.*

*Johnny himself is small and fair-haired. He takes after his paternal grandmother, his mother says....*

40